SUMMER
balloon
bee
butterfly
picnic basket
fan

Find MouseWorks at www.DisneyBooks.com

For information address Disney Press, 114 Fifth Avenue, New York, New York 10011-5690.
Printed in Mexico

First Edition
1 3 5 7 9 10 8 6 4 2
ISBN: 0-7364-0142-3

Disney's

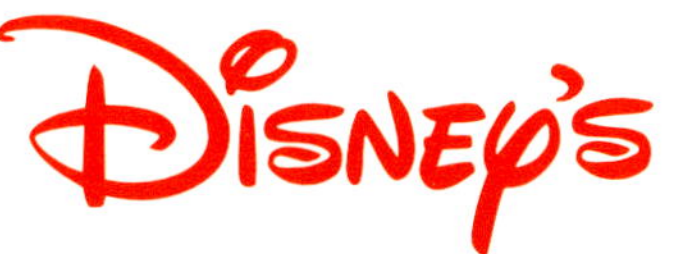

Winnie the Pooh's
Big Book of First Words

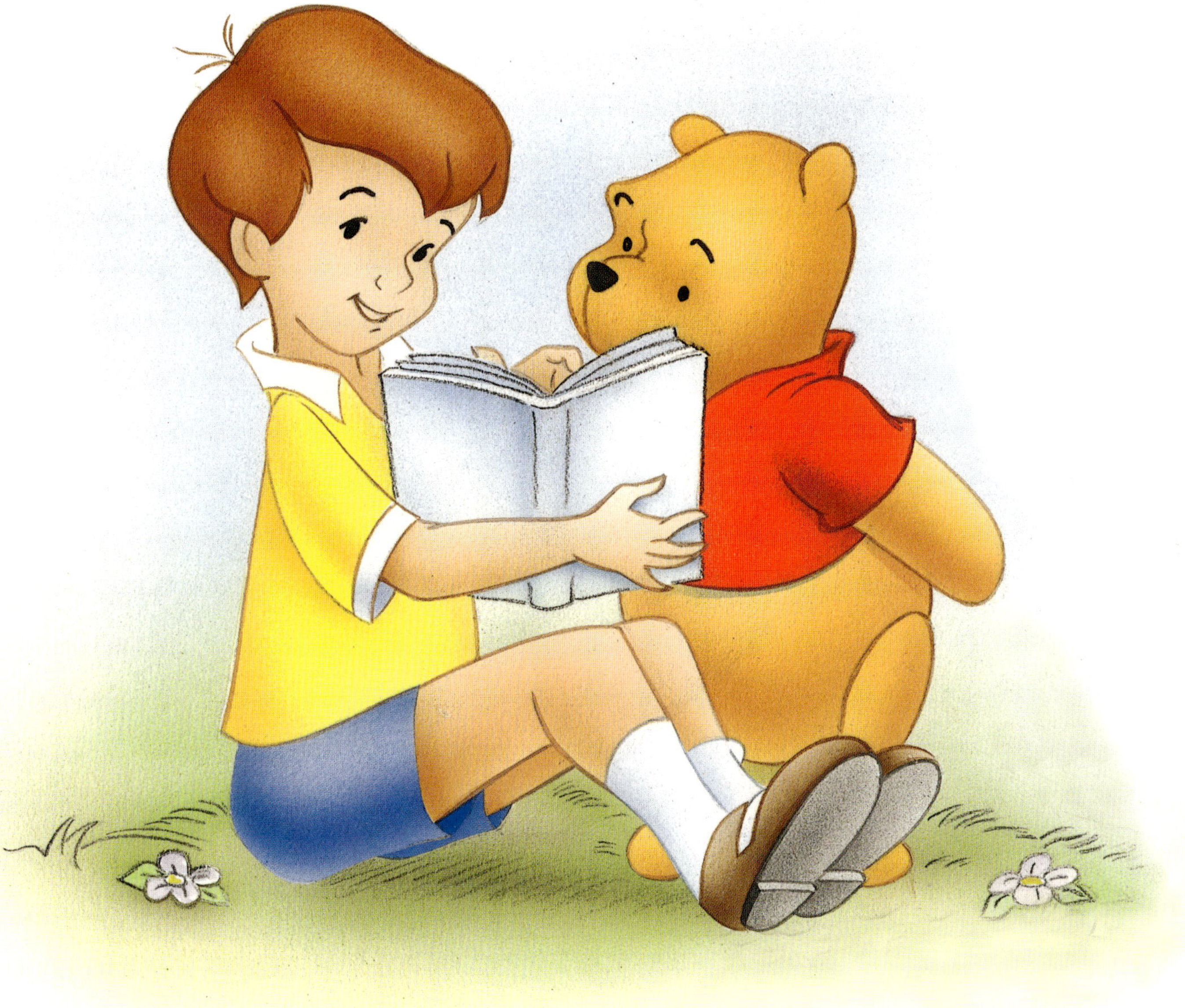

MOUSE WORKS

Kathleen W. Zoehfeld ✿ Illustrated by Josie Yee

New York

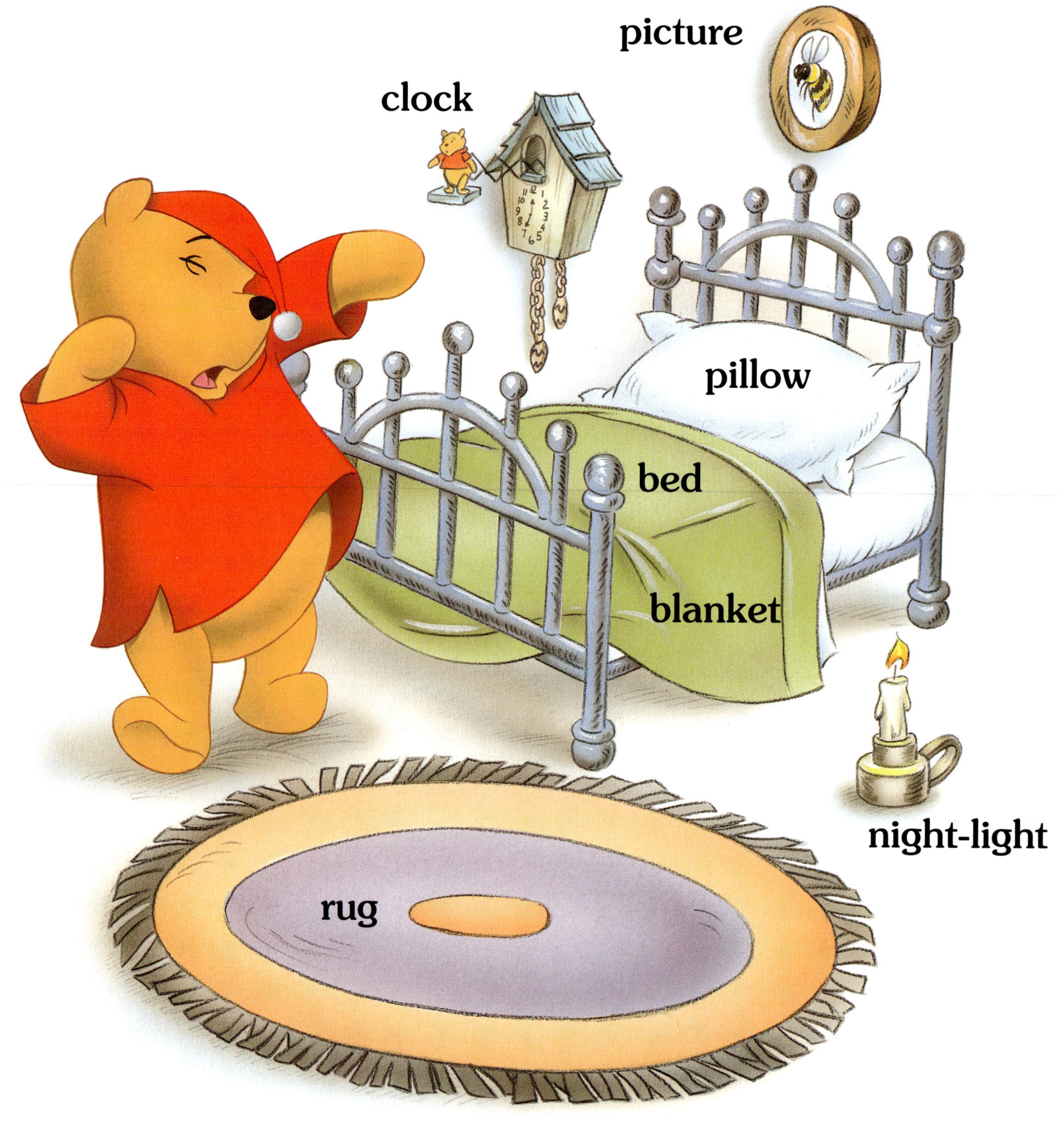

The sun is rising over the Hundred-Acre Wood.
Winnie the Pooh yawns and stretches.

Wake up, sleepy old bear!

curtains
cupboard
sunrise
closet
window
lamp
dresser
vase
milk
broom
table
chair
honeypot

Pooh sings a song as he does his stoutness exercises:

"Bend and stretch . . . Dum de dum . . .
Rum tum tiddle tum . . .
Hum tum tummy!"

Pooh pats his tummy.
"That reminds me.
It's time for a little
something!" he says.

When Pooh feels rumbly in his tummy,
he goes for a walk through the Hundred-Acre Wood.
He always knows where to find honey!

feather
baby birds
bird nest
leaf
branch
tree
chipmunk
bees' nest
twig
honey
bark
tree trunk
rock
squirrel
root
path
bridge
salamander
mud

Oh, dear! Pooh is STILL hungry.

He sees Rabbit working in his garden.

Maybe Rabbit has something else to eat, thinks Pooh.

apples
pears
fence
hoe
rake
green beans
corn
tomatoes
seeds
flowers
wagon
pail
spade

Ding, ding, ding!

"Christopher Robin is ringing his bell!" says Pooh. "Time for everyone to play school!"

Owl
Owl's wing
Tigger
Tigger's stripes
Gopher
Kanga
Eeyore
Roo
Kanga's pouch
Eeyore's tail

"Come on!" calls Christopher Robin.
"Everything is ready."

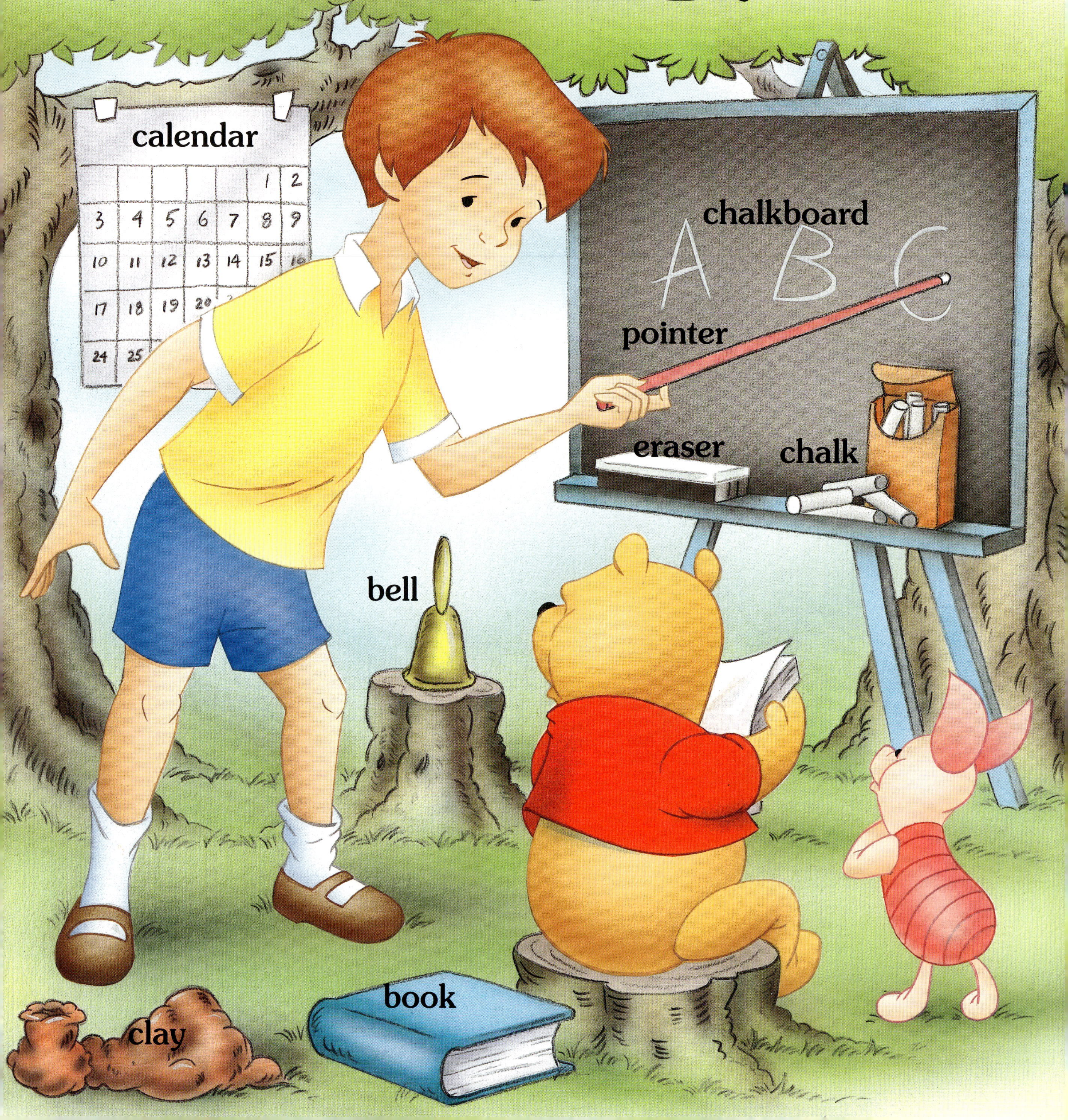

calendar

chalkboard

pointer

eraser

chalk

bell

book

clay

scissors
map
paintbrush
paint
horn
stool
crayons
scrapbook
drum
table
ruler
drumsticks
string
chair
paste
blocks
paper

Pooh loves to look at books at school.
His favorite book is *The Animal ABC.*

"Time to turn
the page," says Roo.

Jj jay
Kk koala
Ll lion
Mm
mouse
Nn newt
Oo octopus
Pp
panther

"The end!" cries Tigger.

Christopher Robin has learned many things at his real school. He likes to teach Pooh about opposites.

Roo's shirt is **dirty.**

Pooh's shirt is **clean.**

Piglet is **small.**

A heffalump is **large.**

Tigger's tail is **long.**

Rabbit's tail is **short.**

Tigger is **happy.**

Eeyore is **sad.**

Eeyore's pot is **empty.**

Pooh's pot is **full.**

Owl has been busy painting. He holds up his work for all to see.

"Can you name the colors in this picture?" he asks.

Rabbit has something to show, too.

"How many different shapes can you find in my picture?" he asks.

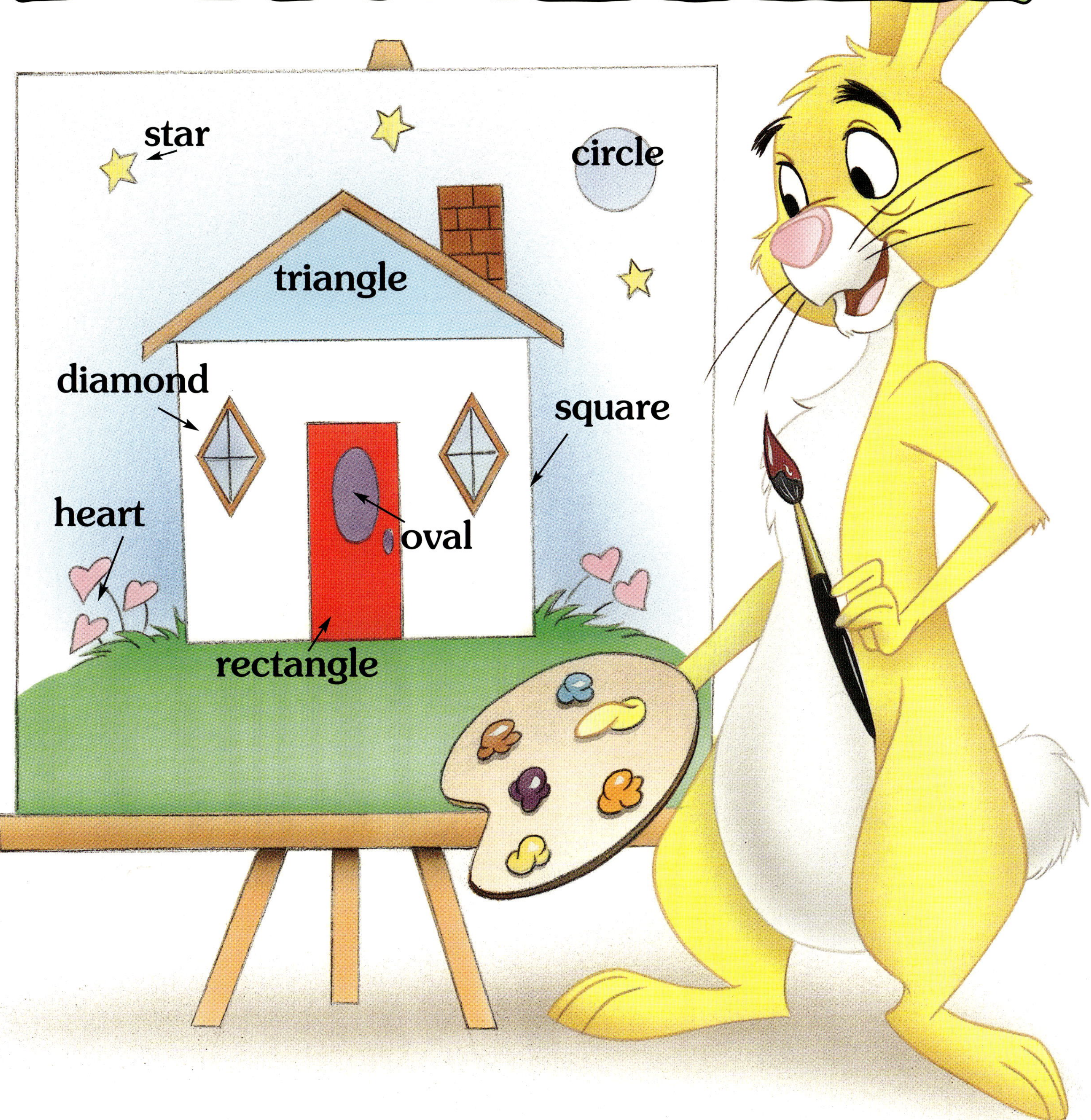

"You've been good students all morning," says Christopher Robin. "Now it's time for recess!"

"Oh, boy!" cries Pooh. He loves to play.

Owl flies.
playhouse
swing
Pooh swings.
Rabbit catches.
Piglet climbs.
seesaw
Eeyore sits.
Roo hops.
hopscotch
jacks

After all that playing, everyone is hungry.

"Look!" calls Pooh. "Kanga has brought a delicious picnic lunch."

emonade
sandwiches
honeypot
bread
ar
pickles
cheese
peach
bananas
boiled eggs
crackers
orange
grapes
watermelon
ants

After lunch, Roo has an idea. "Let's play with Tigger's toys!" he shouts.

"Okay!" agrees Tigger. Tiggers and Roos love things that go!

Piglet and Pooh prefer the quieter toys today.

“Uh-oh! Tigger’s truck is broken.
What can we do?” asks Roo.
“Let’s take it to Gopher’s workshop.
Maybe he can fix it,” says Pooh.
can
wrench
saw
sawhorse
jar
box
nuts
bolts
nails

"All fixed!" says Gopher.
tape measure
toolbox
pliers
file
plane
hammer
workbench
screwdriver
sandpaper

At the end of the day, Kanga invites everyone to her house for supper.

On their way, Pooh and Piglet count:

3
three honey trees
5
five flying birds
4
four buzzing bees
6
six Pooh sticks

8
eight leaves
7
seven
stepping stones
9
pinecones

10
ten strawberries

11
eleven acorns

12
twelve of
Rabbit's small
relations

"Mmmm, something smells yummy," says Pooh.

Kanga is cooking supper in her kitchen. Pooh goes in to see if he can help.

flour
measuring cup
measuring spoons
cake
sink
pitcher
cereal bowl
sugar
bib
teakettle
teacup
table
high chair

brush
medicine
chest
toothbrushes
toothpaste
mirror
faucet
sink
comb
towel
bubble bath
sponge

After Pooh and the others thank Kanga, it's time for them to go home and for Roo to take his bath.

Soon it's time for everyone to put on their pajamas, even Christopher Robin.

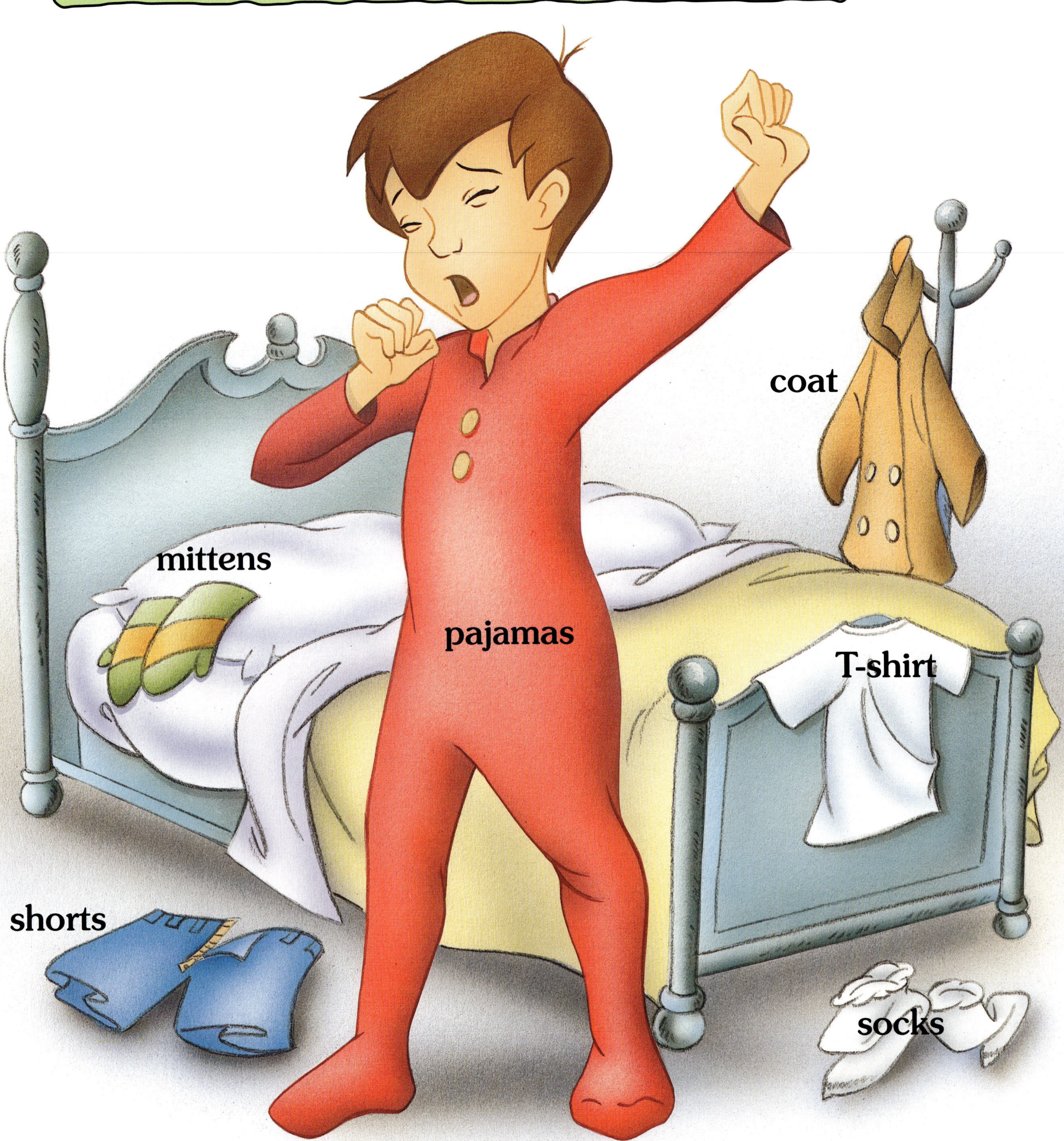

scarf
overalls
sweater
pants
hanger
belt
hat
sneakers
boots
umbrella
shirt
slippers

Good night, all!

Pooh's house
moon
Mr Sanders
sign
star
doorbell
doorknob
sleepy
bear
mailbox
door

FALL
leaves
kite
jack-o'-lantern
pumpkin pie
gourds